Here Comes
Zelda Claus
and Other
Holiday Disasters

Lynn Hall

Here Comes Zelda Claus
and *Other*
Holiday Disasters

Harcourt Brace & Company
San Diego   New York   London

Library of Congress Cataloging-in-Publication Data
Hall, Lynn.
Here comes Zelda Claus, and other holiday disasters/
by Lynn Hall.
p. cm.
Summary: Relates the amusing holiday misadventures
of Zelda Hammersmith, whose good intentions only
lead to trouble.
[1. Holidays—Fiction. 2. Humorous stories.] I. Title.
PZ7.H1458He   1987   [Fic]—dc19   88-27115
ISBN 0-15-233790-3

Designed by Nancy J. Ponichtera
Printed in the United States of America
O N M L K

Contents

Here Comes
Zelda Claus
and Other
Holiday Disasters

1. Zelda, the Death of the Party

I'm Zelda Hammersmith. Maybe you've heard of me: Zelda, the life of the party. Well, that's what they used to call me, anyway. Before last Halloween. I'm not sure what they're calling me now. Probably "that crazy girl with the weird underwear."

My best friend, Kimberley, was at my house one night a couple of weeks before Halloween. It's not really a house—it's a trailer in Perfect Paradise Trailer Park on the edge of town. Mom and I have been living there ever since my dad went to Nashville to try to make it big as a country music singer.

I don't know why Kimberley is my best friend. She's skinny and dark-haired, and so neat and clean she makes me sick. Her hair never moves, and she never sits on the floor. I'm much more lovable. I'm sort of chunky like a teddy bear, with curly hair the color of cookie dough. And I don't believe in wasting my energy staying clean—I've got more important things to do.

Kimberley was sitting cleanly on the sofa and I was on the floor looking through an old coloring book when the phone rang. We were watching "Dallas" on television, and Mom always cusses under her breath if the phone rings during "Dallas." She's in love with J.R., if you ask me.

It must have been a pretty good phone call because she reached around the corner with her toe and turned down the TV so she could hear better, and she talked for a long time. Kimberly leaned forward and tried to lip-read what the actors on the screen were saying. I went back to studying my coloring book.

It was an old one I'd colored up a long time ago, but it was all Halloween pictures and I was looking for ideas. In a couple of weeks it would be trick-or-treat time, and I wanted a super costume this year. I was tired of cutting holes in a sheet and being a ghost.

My theory was that if you have a terrific costume and look adorable in it, you can get up to twice as much candy as somebody who just makes circles on his face with lipstick, like some of the kids do. I'm getting up to the dangerous age where the little kids look cuter than me, especially Derek. He's the littlest kid in the trailer park and his mother makes adorable costumes for him. It was going to take some planning to out-cute Derek.

Finally Mom hung up and came back to sit with us. You'd like my mom.

She's just like me, only bigger. She was wearing her usual jeans, a gray sweatshirt that said *Keep on Truckin'*, and a pair of socks I gave her. They were red and orange and pink and green and purple striped, and they had separate toes, like gloves. She says they're her favorite socks, and I can see why.

Without even turning up the TV so she could hear J.R., she flopped down in her chair and said, "How would you girls like a neighborhood Halloween party this year?"

Kimberley and I looked at each other.

"Will it have good refreshments?" I asked.

"Can we wear costumes?" Kimberley asked, probably thinking about her butterfly costume. She takes ballet lessons AND tap dance lessons, and she never lets me forget it. Her butterfly costume from her recital is her favorite possession.

Mom tipped up her can and finished off her Mountain Dew. "That was Derek's mother on the phone. She's getting some parents together, and we're going to have a neighborhood Halloween party for you kids, over at the armory. She wanted me to help out with the committees."

"I'll help," I said fast, before Kimberley could beat me to it.

"Thanks, dumpling."

Kimberley said, "What will they have for us to do at the party?"

"Oh, the usual," Mom said. "Some games, prizes for the best costume, stuff like that. We're going to have the party so you kids won't have to go trick-or-treating. That's getting kind of dangerous, and some of the mothers don't want their kids out running around at night in costumes. You remember that boy in the skeleton costume who almost got hit by a car last year."

"Aww," I whined. "Can't I go trick-or-treating? I was going to think up a really great costume this year."

I hated to give up trick-or-treating. Last year I kept track of who gave what, so this year I knew where to go for popcorn balls and caramel apples. And I knew the places to avoid, where they gave one stick of spearmint gum.

I hugged Mom's legs and gave her my most adorable pleading look. It didn't work.

"Knock it off, Zelda. You'll have the party instead of trick-or-treating, you'll get just as sick on party refreshments, and you won't have to go tromping all over the neighborhood falling over your costume. And get this: Guess what the prize for the best costume is going to be?"

"A gift certificate for the Young Fashions Shop," Kimberley chirped.

"A pony!" I yelled. Might as well start guessing from the top down, and a pony was the ultimate prize.

Mom winked at me and said, "Smaller."

"A dog!"

"Smaller."

"Hamster."

"Bigger."

The way her eyes twinkled, I suddenly knew. Gripping my hands over my heart, I said, "A long-haired guinea pig with swirls in its coat!"

"Yes!" Mom laughed at the joy all over my face, but then sobered a little when she noticed Kimberley's expression. Gift certificates for clothes would have been more her style.

But for me, a long-haired guinea pig was right up there with ponies. I'd been wanting one forever—since last summer, when I'd seen one in the pet shop in the mall. Mom knew how much I wanted one. She must have suggested it as a prize. A happy thought struck me.

"Who's going to be the judge of the costume contest? You?" I asked. If Mom was going to be the judge, I was in!

"Of course not," she said sternly. "We'll pick somebody for the judge who doesn't have a child in the contest. You wouldn't want to win unfairly, would you?"

Yes. I would. I wanted to win any old way I could.

Kimberley got a dreamy smile on her face and said, "I'll wear my butterfly costume."

"Surprise, surprise," I muttered.

"If I win," she went on, "I could always trade the guinea pig for something I wanted. What are you going to go as, Zelda? A ghost again, like last year?"

"I don't know yet," I said, kind of snooty. "I'll have to think about it. But don't worry, it'll be something amazing."

Mom gave me a warning look.

◎

All the next week I thought about my costume. I made a list of everything I could think of that was Halloweeny. Ghost—too common and boring. Witch—too common, and I didn't have the face for it. I was too round and rosy-cheeked. Now, Kimberley would have been a good witch, but she'd never mess up her perfect face with a long fake nose that had warts on it.

Skeleton—too common and boring. Pumpkin—too hard to run around in, and impossible to eat in. Black cat? Possibly . . . maybe . . . but not quite good enough.

Then it hit me. BAT. That would be perfect. Bats were Halloweeny and yucky and sickening. Ideal. All I'd need would be something to make me look black and skinny and winged and claw-footed. That wouldn't be hard at all.

That night Mom and I went through everything in both of our closets and the linen closet, trying to find black stuff to make a bat out of me.

"I'm sorry, dumpling," she said finally. "Black just isn't my color. All I've got is that one skirt, and you can't have that. I know what. Let's call Cindy and ask her. She wears lots of black and she's got enough clothes to choke a horse." She went right to the phone and dialed.

Cindy is Mom's best friend. Mom works as a sausage stuffer in a packing plant, and Cindy works there, too. She's funny. She thinks she's beautiful, and she has boyfriends all over the place who get tangled up with ex-husbands. She wears so much mascara that her eyes look like caterpillars.

Cindy told Mom to come on over. She had a date, but he was boring and she'd have more fun making a bat out of me than she was having with the boy-friend. So we hurried up and drove over to her apartment.

When we got there, I could tell right away that Cindy wasn't going to keep this boyfriend much longer. For one thing, she was wearing loose slacks and a big sloppy shirt. The more she likes a guy, the tighter the clothes she wears.

And he didn't look like her type.

Darrell, his name was. He was huge and had an orange beard that spread way out, and a bald head with wild fringes of hair around the edges. About all I could see of his face was his fat red lips and little beady eyes glaring down at me.

"How long is this going to take?" he asked Cindy when she introduced us.

"Quite a while," she told him in a breezy voice. "Come on back here—let's see what we can find that might work."

We all went into her bedroom and stood around while she opened the closet door, which was one whole wall, and started pitching black things out onto the bed. Darrell stood in the door-way clenching a beer can in his fist.

I said, "I'll need to look black all over, and real skinny, and I'll need great big wings."

Out flew two skirts.

"I'll need black claw feet," I added. Out flew sweatpants and a winter coat.

"And a black head," Mom said.

Darrell grunted.

"This might work." Cindy fought her way out of the closet, waving a fancy black dress over her head. When she held it up to her body, I could see that it was a genuine all-out dress-up dress—skinny and shiny black, with little sparklies all over it.

Cindy glanced over at Darrell. "You might as well leave, Darrell. This is probably going to take all evening. No use you hanging around."

"Come on, Cin," he whined. "I thought we were going to go out tonight."

"This is more important. I have to turn my best friend's only child into a bat before this weekend. I can go out with you any time."

If I'd been him, I wouldn't have stood still for that. I'd have marched right out of there. But he just drooped against the doorway, looking sad and belching.

I took the dress and held it up to me. It poked out in front, just as if I had a real chest. I didn't know whether bats had bosoms, but I thought maybe no one would notice.

Cindy went to the bedroom door and closed it, just missing Darrell's fingers and beard. "Okay for you, Cindy," he bellowed through the door.

We stripped off my clothes and got me into the dress, laughing at the way it looked on me. There was a lot of dress left over, past my feet. I thought it made me look more like a shrunken movie star than a bat, but Mom and Cindy walked around me, squeezing their lips between their fingers and going "hmmm" a lot.

"If we took off the flounce down the back . . . ," Cindy muttered.

"There's enough material around the bottom to make wings," Mom said.

Cindy stared at me for a long time, thinking. Then, with a whoop, she started pawing through the dresser drawers.

"Here—try these over your head."

She handed me a pair of black tights. "They've got a hole in one heel," she said. "Here—just slip them on over your head, and we'll tie the legs around your neck. You can see and breathe right through them. There—that's terrific."

She and Mom both fell on the bed, they were laughing so hard. The tights flattened my nose and lips, but I could breathe okay, and I could see well enough to get around, although the world was gray.

"Hey, wait a minute," I yelled suddenly through the tights. "How can I eat with these on?"

"No problem," Mom said. "The committee decided to have the costume competition first thing, because there'll be lots of kids who won't be able to eat or play games very well in their costumes. So after the judging, you can just take the tights off your head."

That sounded good to me. "Now, what about my feet?"

From the living room, Darrell bellowed, "If you don't come out of there, I'm leaving, Cindy. I'm going down to the Dew Drop without you."

"Fine," she called back.

The three of us stared at my feet some more. "Ho!" Cindy cried, jumping up from the bed and punching Mom's leg. "I've got it! I've got perfect bats' feet for her."

She dug around in dresser drawers some more and came up with a pair of long, black dress-up gloves, the kind that come clear up your arm. I couldn't walk in the dress, so she picked me up and sat me on the bed, and when she and Mom found my feet under the long dress, they pulled the gloves on and jerked them up to my knees.

I stood up. The hand part of the

gloves stuck out in front of my toes, just exactly like bat claws. That Cindy wasn't as dumb as she looked.

"I'm leaving," Darrell yelled through the door.

"Fine. 'Bye," we all called back.

Mom got me out of the dress, Cindy opened up her sewing machine, and they went to work on the dress. After a while I got bored watching them and went out to the living room to play slap-jack with Darrell, who was still there. He didn't know how to play. I had to show him.

"Some date," he said once, right after I slapjacked his cards and beat him again.

I shrugged and smiled. "I'm having fun," I said.

◎

Party day finally arrived. The party was going to start at seven on Saturday night. I went over to the armory with

Mom and two other moms right after lunch to help put up decorations.

The National Guard Armory was right next to the trailer park, so we just walked over. It was a big, tan, brick building with a hollow, echoing sound inside. We went into the main room and stood looking around.

The big, empty room was like our school gym when the lunch tables aren't folded out from the walls. Only this room had things parked along one wall—a jeep and a big brownish-green truck with canvas over the back, just like a covered wagon.

An army guy came out of a little room at the side and walked over to us.

Mom said, "Can you move those trucks out of here? We need to get our party decorations up. I'm Mrs. Hammersmith—I talked to you on the phone about using the building tonight for the kids' Halloween party, remember?"

He was very polite. "I know, and I'm

sorry about the jeep and the truck. I forgot about them when I talked to you. They're both down for repairs, and we can't drive either one of them; otherwise we could have backed them out for the night. I'm afraid you'll just have to make do with the space available."

Mom looked at Mrs. Curtiss, Kimberley's mom, and they shrugged. "We'll still have plenty of room," Mom said. "Is it okay if we go ahead and put up streamers and stuff like that?"

He waved us on and brought out a tall stepladder and some folding tables. The moms put me to work twisting orange and black streamers together and blowing up spooky-face black balloons. I was glad it was Saturday afternoon and Kimberley had dance lessons. It was fun being the only kid helper.

While I watched Mrs. Curtiss hanging streamers from the light fixtures and looping them across the ceiling, I started thinking.

I thought about my bat costume,

which was pretty good and might win the long-haired guinea pig.

Then I thought about Kimberley fluttering around in her butterfly outfit looking beautiful. I thought about Derek in the giant pumpkin he'd worn last year for trick-or-treating, when he'd gotten twice as much candy as the rest of us because he couldn't get through people's doors and they felt sorry for him.

I thought about Derek in the cute fuzzy rabbit costume his mother had made him last Easter, with the big floppy feet. Even *I* thought he was adorable in that, and I don't even like him.

I've just got to win, I thought. *I need something more than just a good costume. I need . . .*

And then I had it. My Plan!

I ran over to where Mom and Derek's mom were taping cardboard skeletons to the walls.

"I have a great idea for the costume contest," I said.

"A little higher," Mom said. "Now to the right—more . . . more . . . there. That's perfect."

"Mom." I danced and poked at her.

"What?" she growled.

"I have an idea for the costume contest. How about if you turn off all the lights and have each person come out, one at a time, and have like a spotlight just on that one kid?"

Mom and Derek's mom stopped taping, to think. Mrs. Curtiss, on the ladder, paused with the end of the streamers in her mouth. I could see her picturing her beautiful Kimberley fluttering into the spotlight. I could see Derek's mom picturing an adorable little rabbit or pumpkin having the spotlight all to himself. I could see Mom wondering what I was up to.

"That's a good idea," Mrs. Curtiss said. "We've got a high-powered camping lantern I could bring for the spotlight."

Cackling softly to myself, I danced

away to look for the next thing I was going to need.

I found the nice man in the side room and said, "Would you happen to have some rope we could use? A skinny rope, about twenty feet long?"

He thought a while, then said, "I think there's some sash cord back in the storeroom. Take a look, back through that door over there. You can use it— just don't cut it up."

I followed his pointing finger through a big kitchen-type room to the storeroom. I found the cord coiled on top of a pile of rifle targets. It was perfect—thick enough to hold my weight, skinny enough not to be noticed. I wadded it up and carried it casually behind my back into the main room, then dropped it behind the truck.

I waited and waited for all three moms to be looking the other way at the same time, but they kept moving around, decorating things.

Finally I said, "There's a kitchen

over here and a coffeepot. Should I make you some coffee?"

"No!" Mom bellowed. "Don't touch a thing. You'll burn the place down, Zelda."

But Mrs. Curtiss came down from her ladder rubbing the back of her neck. "I don't know about the rest of you, but I'm ready for a break. Let's go check out the coffee situation."

Yay, hurray!

As soon as they were all out of sight, I grabbed the rope, scooted up the ladder, and tied the rope around the chain that the light fixture was hanging from. I tied a double double knot, then scrambled down the ladder, took the other end of the rope, and draped it across the top of the huge army truck. It showed up, but not as much as the orange and black streamers did.

It looked to me like Mrs. Curtiss was finished at that light fixture anyway. I dragged the ladder over to the next one.

The moms came out of the kitchen

then, and from what they were muttering, I guessed there must not have been
any coffee or coffeepot in the kitchen
after all.

Mrs. Curtiss looked startled seeing
where the ladder was, but she climbed
it anyway and started hanging more
streamers.

I was safe! Hurray! And that long-
haired guinea pig was in the bag.

◎

I was almost too excited to eat any supper that night. Cindy came over at five
and brought my finished bat costume.
She said she'd given up a chance to go
out with Darrell to come and see the bat
costume on me. I had to agree—there
was no comparison between Darrell and
Zelda the Bat.

I tried on the costume while Mom
stirred up sloppy joes for supper. It was
perfect. Cindy had taken the ruffles off
the back and made it tight down over
my legs. She'd made sleeve things that

were kind of like a cape; they covered the bare top part of me and hid the two empty bosom cups in front.

Then, because I'd wanted the wings to be longer than my arms, she'd broken a yardstick in half and sewed the pieces into the tips of the wings. I had to hold the ends in my hands to make them aim right, but they made the wings perfect and batty. The black material hung from the wing tips to my hips, and when I raised my arms I was positive I could fly.

Then I pulled the black tights down over my face, wrapped the legs around my neck, and flew to the kitchen making bat noises. Mom jumped two feet off the floor and almost spilled the sloppy joes.

After supper I took a bath and got dressed in my favorite orange sweat suit with *Zelda* written across the top in big pink letters. I even put on my Spider-woman underpants because they had pictures all around of Spiderwoman flying through the air. I thought they might help get me in the mood when I made my grand entrance.

We stuffed the costume in a shopping bag and walked over to the armory. The big room really did look like a Halloween party, with all the orange and black crepe paper streamers making a tent of the ceiling.

Casually, acting as cool as I could, I strolled over by the truck and looked up. Whew. My rope was still there, hanging from the light fixture and looping over to the top of the truck. With all the streamers, I wouldn't have noticed it if I hadn't put it there myself.

Kimberley came over to me eating a square of chocolate-and-orange cake. She didn't even have frosting on her fingers. I didn't know that was possible.

"I asked my brother," she said, "and he promised to buy the guinea pig from me for ten dollars."

I looked down my nose at her. "Huh. You have to win it first."

"Oh, sure. But I've been going around asking everybody what their costume is, and there isn't any competition. Brinda is going to be a witch, Jason's a hobo, Derek is going to do that stupid pumpkin thing again."

"Didn't you forget somebody?" I glared.

"Oh, yes. Sorry. What are you dressing as, Zelda—a bed sheet ghost again?"

"Wait and see," I snipped, and walked away. Boy, would she ever see.

It took about half an hour of boring, time-killing stuff before the committee decided we were all there. Then, when I didn't think I could stand it any longer, Mrs. Curtiss stood in the middle of the room and clapped her hands.

"All right now, boys and girls. Time to get started on the costume contest. Now, right over there"—she pointed to the corner near my truck—"through that door in the corner is a room where you can change into your costumes.

Then we're going to turn off the lights, and I want you to walk out here to the middle of the floor one at a time as I call your names. We're going to turn a spotlight on you as you come out, just like they do with movie stars."

People around me breathed in and whispered. I could tell they liked the idea of being in the spotlight one at a time. *Just wait*, I thought, bouncing on one foot.

Mrs. Curtiss went on. "Our judge tonight will be Mrs. Birdsall"—applause, applause—"and as you probably already know, the prize is this fine guinea pig over here on the corner table."

I'd already visited him. He was beautiful. He looked something like a furry slipper. His hair was long and it grew in funny swirls all over his body, with the swirls crowding each other and standing straight out. All you could see of his face were his beady black eyes and a shiny little nose. I decided to name him Mr. Batman, and I was prepared to love him forever.

I wasn't sure whether having Mrs. Birdsall as the judge would be lucky for me or not. She was a tall, skinny lady who lived in the trailer next door and took care of me after school. I could never tell whether she actually liked me or not.

Mom and Cindy came over and hugged me for good luck, and I ran to the changing room with my bag of bat. Mom and Cindy wanted to come too and help, but I wouldn't let them. That could ruin my plan.

The room was crowded with kids and moms struggling with costumes. Derek's pumpkin took up half the space. I had to hide behind a stack of boxes to get into the dress so people wouldn't see me in my underwear. Derek's mom had to zip me up the back.

"What are you, dear?" she asked. "A witch, I bet."

I didn't say anything. She'd get the

idea as soon as she saw me soaring into the spotlight.

"Don't touch my wings, don't touch my wings," Kimberley yelped. Butterfly wings are harder to take care of than bat wings. I just folded mine at my sides and waited until the last minute to put on the hood and feet.

From the room beyond, Mrs. Curtiss yelled, "Okay, are you ready? First is Brinda Burgess."

The room got black, and Brinda ran out into the spotlight. Cheers, applause.

"Next, Aron Thompson." Aron gathered up his tiger tail and ran out.

I leaned against the stack of boxes and struggled into the long gloves that ran up my legs and made beautiful bat claws out in front of my toes.

"Next, Kimberley Curtiss." I could hear her mother raising the roof cheering and applauding as the butterfly toe-danced, dipping and twirling, into the spotlight. She swooped back and forth for almost a minute while the poor spot-light person kept losing her.

I pulled the tights down over my face and wrapped the legs loosely around my neck.

"Next, Zelda Hammersmith." Applause, applause. I ran through the door, ducked to the right, and began climbing up onto the truck. That is not easy when you have gloves hanging from your feet.

"Next, Zelda Hammersmith," the voice called again.

"Coming," I yelled, trying to make my voice sound like it was coming from the dressing room.

Finally I got a good hold and rolled up onto the canvas top of the truck. There was my rope. I grabbed it and made a slipknot loop, dropping it over my head and shoulders.

But . . . I couldn't get my wings through.

"Next, Zelda Hammersmith!" The voice sounded crabby now.

Thrashing frantically, I struggled to get my arms up through the loop. As I turned sideways, my foot got caught on my other foot's glove and I fell.

Out over the edge of the truck I swung. The rope tightened with a jerk, pinning my arms to my sides. Light flashed in my eyes as I swung through the spotlight.

On the return swing, I felt myself turning over. Oh, no. My head hung straight down, my feet stuck straight up with their glove hands dangling. Back and forth I swung, in and out of the spotlight.

When I finally came to a stop, it was in the full glare of the spotlight. The legs of the tights had come unwound from my neck and hung straight down, their toes pointed outward.

The black dress came slithering down my body, uncovering my underpants. My Spiderwoman underpants.

Just when things couldn't get any worse, they did. My rope gave a little jerk. Bits of ceiling dropped past my face. There was a ripping noise, a flash and a pop, and all of a sudden every light in the building went out.

I was dropping lower! Mom got to me just as my head touched the floor.

◎

Actually, it turned out to be a good party in spite of me. The armory man was pretty mad at first when he got there and found the light fixture ripped loose from the ceiling and hanging by one chain. When the wires had broken, they had short-circuited all the lights in the building.

But after looking into the situation for a while and listening to me and Mom apologizing over and over, he finally told us that their insurance would probably cover bat-children swinging from light fixtures.

"I've got one like that at home my-self," he said to Mom, looking down at me with a glum look. I had the feeling he was sorry for Mom.

We had the rest of the party by candlelight, which was just right for a Halloween party anyhow. They even let me make another entrance into the spotlight, walking this time, and just flapping my wings once or twice. I kept thinking about all those people seeing me in my underwear.

Then we played games by candlelight and told ghost stories, and finally we walked home. Mom and Cindy were up in front, muttering about stupid, dangerous tricks and how I could have killed myself.

I promised not ever to do anything dumb again in my whole life.

Then I looked down at Mr. Batman in his cage under my wing and winked at him.

He winked back.

2. Thanks a Lot, Zelda

Mom taught me a song as we drove along. " 'Over the river and through the woods, to Grandmother's house we go.' " And then some more about horses and sleighs. It was old-fashioned music and it didn't have much of a beat, but Mom had so much fun singing it that I got into the mood, too.

We were on our way, over the river and through the woods, to Grandmother's house for Thanksgiving. Mom got off work early on Wednesday afternoon and picked me up at school, and we were off.

She warned me that it was going to be a long drive—about four hours, unless the weather got bad. Then it would be more. Usually I hated long drives because my body wasn't designed to sit still on car seats for more than ten minutes. But I was excited about this trip.

"You'll be meeting lots of relatives you haven't seen since you were little," Mom told me as we drove. "You probably don't remember Uncle Bill and Aunt Jill and your cousins, Buffy, Muffy, and Duffy."

"Sounds like a litter of kittens," I said.

"Yes, well, don't say that to them. The children will be too young for you to have much fun with, I'm afraid. They're four, three, and teeny."

I shot her a dark look from the corner of my eye. "Am I going to have to take care of them and read them stories and boring stuff like that?"

"If you're asked to," she said in her hard voice. "I'm sure you'll be a gracious guest and help in any way you can, without griping or muttering. Won't you, Zelda." It wasn't a question.

I said, "What other relatives will be there?"

"Nobody else. Oh, just Gramma Zee. Do you remember her? It's her house, so naturally she'll be there."

"If it's her house, how come Uncle Bill and Aunt Jill and all those Uffies live there?"

"Uffies? Oh, you mean Buffy, Muffy, and Duffy. Don't call them Uffies to their faces, will you? They live there because Uncle Bill takes care of the farm for Gramma Zee. Her husband died a long time ago, so Bill and Jill came to live there and take care of the farm and Gramma."

"Is she mine or yours?" I asked.

Mom said, "She's my grandmother, your great-grandmother. Bill is my brother and your uncle. Jill is my sister-in-law and your aunt. The . . . uh . . . the Uffies are your cousins and my nieces and nephew. Got all that straight?"

"Sure," I lied. Of course I understood grandparents and brothers, but I still got a little confused about things like cousins and nephews.

We didn't really drive over the river and through the woods, like the song said. It was more over the freeway and through the night, with a stop for supper at a truck plaza on the interstate.

It was a great restaurant, with one whole section for truck drivers only. I got up and walked around and looked at the truck drivers to see what made them so special. I stared at them and they stared back at me. I couldn't see anything special about them.

Then I went over to where they sold stuff and started looking at it. The postcards had cartoons on them, but I didn't understand most of them. I guess they were adult cartoons. I picked up an ash-tray that had a funny little man sitting on the edge, with a naked rear end. I had just started reading the bottom of the ashtray—"Put your old butts here"—when Mom came over and jerked me away by the hood of my parka.

After supper we kept on driving. It was dark by then, and we were off the interstate and on a narrow highway that went through little towns about every ten minutes. It started snowing, first with great big soft flakes that looked like torn Kleenex, then with smaller, faster flakes. Mom leaned for-ward and concentrated on driving.

Finally, when I was sure I couldn't sit one more minute with my feet dan-gling, Mom said, "Ah, there's the road to the farm. Now listen, dumpling, you will be on your best behavior while we're here, won't you? We'll be leaving tomor-row after the big Thanksgiving dinner, so you'll only have to be good tonight and tomorrow morning. You can manage that, can't you?"

I was wounded to my heart. "I'm always good. Aren't I?"

"Well, Zelda, your intentions are always good. Usually. But sometimes your judgment is, shall we say, flawed. Sometimes you get ideas—one might say *harebrained* ideas—and you know what the results can be."

I didn't have an answer for that.

"So all I'm saying is, I know you're a wonderful child, and you know you're a wonderful child. What I'd like to do now is just . . ."

She couldn't think of a polite way of saying it, so I helped her. "Fool the rest of them into thinking I never get into trouble. Right?"

"Well, something like that."

That wouldn't be too hard, I thought as we bumped along a country road. It was only natural that Mom would want to show me off. I was her kid and she was raising me all alone. I made up my mind to be incredibly good for the next twenty-four hours.

◎

We slowed way down by a mailbox that stood on its own leg, then we turned into a narrow, bumpy track, and there was the house. It looked like a happy house, with big evergreen trees hugging its corners and orange paths of light coming out from its windows. Snow drifted through the light streaks and made them beautiful.

The door opened and people came out and hugged Mom and me, helping us carry our stuff inside. I was going to carry in the Jell-O Mom had made in the shape of a turkey, but she grabbed it out of my hands. She was right. I probably would have tripped and fallen in it, and then she wouldn't be able to show me off.

Finally we were all inside on a porch, stomping our feet and taking off boots and jackets. Mom talked about where we'd run into the snow and how the roads were.

Then the final step, from the porch into the kitchen, where we all stood around in a kind of circle, and Mom introduced me. "Zelda, this is Uncle Bill, Aunt Jill, and your cousin Muffy."

"Buffy," Aunt Jill corrected.

"Sorry. Buffy, and Duffy, and the baby is . . ."

"Muffy," everyone said together.

Uncle Bill was a great big man with a red face and yellow hair, eyebrows, and eyelashes. He looked like he smiled and laughed a lot, whether he knew what he was laughing about or not.

Aunt Jill looked teeny and skinny beside him. She had long straight hair and a tired smile. The baby in her arms was eating a fistful of her hair and drooling in it. I decided not to have any babies.

The two little kids each had their arms around one of Uncle Bill's legs.

They stared at me like I was from a science fiction movie. I wondered how Uncle Bill walked, with a kid hanging around each leg. It would have to be a duck waddle.

Mom went on. "And honey, this is Great-Gramma Zee. You haven't seen her since you were a little baby. Hi, Gramma." She bent down and hugged the old lady while I tried to take in the oddness of someone as big and old as Mom having a gramma.

Then Gramma Zee came over to me, but she didn't hug me like the rest of them had. She stood and looked at me, and I looked at her. Something told me right then that if I got a hug from her, it would be because she wanted to give it, not just because everybody else had.

She was the littlest adult I'd ever seen. In fact, I hardly had to bend my head back at all to look her in the eye. Her skin was all soft and wrinkly, and it sort of hung down from her bones. Her eyes were such a light blue that they

were almost white, and they were water-
ing, but not with tears. Her lips looked
sunk into her face, and her hair was
almost bald on the top of her head.

She looked me up and down a cou-
ple of times. "So. You're Zelda. I've heard
some stories about you, girl."

I glanced at Mom. "They're not true.
I really didn't do any of those things."

They all laughed, like I was kidding.

As we started into the living room,
Gramma Zee walked beside me. "My
name is Zelda, too," she whispered,
poking me. "Did your mama tell you?
She named you after me."

I stopped and stared. "I never knew
that. I thought there was only one of
me."

"There is, you ignorant child. One
of you, one of me. It doesn't mean we're
anything alike, just because we have the
same name. My dead husband always
said there was never another like me,
and there never would be. You ever get
into any trouble?"

I thought about what Mom had said, and lied as hard as I could. "Nope." I shook my head.

Gramma Zee fell backward into a big deep chair, and then couldn't get her feet up on the stool in front of it. I grabbed her ankles and helped. Aunt Jill disappeared to put the Uffies in bed, now that they'd gotten a look at Mom and me. Uncle Bill and Mom sat on the sofa and started talking about some big football game they were going to watch tomorrow.

Gramma Zee had to breathe a minute before she could go on talking. I could see now why her mouth sank in— she didn't have any teeth. I'd never seen naked gums before. I couldn't stop staring while she talked.

"Well," she said with her lips flopping, "when I was your age I spent more time in the woodshed than in my own bed."

I looked confused, so she said,

"Woodshed was where you went to get paddled back then. Your generation gets psychology instead. Give me a good paddling any day. It's fast, it's honest, and it's over in five minutes."

I was beginning to like this old lady, even if she was using my name. "What did you get paddled for?"

"Anything I could think of."

I nodded, understanding.

"Set fire to the outhouse once, when Dad was in it. That's an outdoor toilet, in case you didn't know. Got a paddling for that. Another time . . ."

"Come along, Gramma," Aunt Jill said. She held out her hand and started pulling Gramma Zee out of the chair.

"I want to finish my story," Gramma yelled.

"It's your bedtime. Come along like a good girl and we'll get you ready for bed."

I watched sadly as Aunt Jill led her away. I had a feeling Gramma Zee wasn't very happy, and I made up my mind to find some way of fixing that.

◎

Mom slept on the sofa in the living room and I slept on the floor in my blue-checked sleeping bag. I woke up early in the morning when Uncle Bill came through on his way outside.

I got up and pulled on my orange sweatpants and my big fuzzy boots and my pink parka with the fur around the hood. It was brand new and too big for me this year. The hood came clear down over my face, so I had to lean my head way back to see.

I went out the back door and stopped to look around from under my hood. It was sunny and glittery and beautiful out, with all the new snow to make tracks in. When I looked all around a circle, I could only see two other houses besides ours, and they were way off down the road. It was funny to think about living in a place like this, with no neighbors ten feet away in all directions. No yelling or traffic or noise at all hardly, except for some animals moaning in the barn.

I followed Uncle Bill's footprints across the yard and down the hill to the barn, then in through the door.

It was almost the biggest building I'd ever been in, except for school. There was a big wide hallway down the middle, with pens of animals and piles of junk everywhere. Along one side of the hallway, a row of cows stood with their tail ends out in the hall and their necks caught in metal traps. They didn't seem to mind the traps, though. They were eating their breakfasts while Uncle Bill fastened huge machines to their bellies to suck the milk out of them.

He showed me what he was doing and how the milk came out of the cows and ran through pipes in the ceiling. At least that's what he told me. I wasn't sure I believed him. It sounded like a pretty strange way to get milk. I asked him why he didn't just buy it in the store like everybody else, but he didn't have time to explain.

I left him alone and went exploring around the barn. I headed for the dark corners first, since that's where the best stuff usually is.

Over in the darkest corner I found something good. It looked like a huge giant sled with a curvy front and a seat with brown leather cushions. The main body of it was painted black with little red lines like racing stripes, and the two metal runners that curved under it had some old red paint still on them.

I knew what it was. It was a sleigh, like the ones you see on television with horses pulling them. There's always a sleigh full of singers in fur robes on those Christmas specials hosted by John Denver or somebody like that.

I ran back to Uncle Bill and yelled, "Hey, Uncle Bill." He was washing off a cow's belly, and when I yelled, the cow jumped sideways and landed on Uncle Bill's foot.

"Sorry," I muttered. I was supposed to be good so Mom could show me off. Luckily she wasn't up yet.

When Uncle Bill got finished rubbing his foot and counting under his breath, I tried again, but without the yelling this time. "Could we go for a sleigh ride, Uncle Bill?"

I pointed to the sleigh in the corner, because he looked confused.

"Nah, we haven't used that thing since I was a kid. Don't have a horse to pull it, and I reckon the harness is all rat-chewed and rotten by now."

"Oh." I drooped pitifully, but it didn't do any good so I went back to the house.

After breakfast there wasn't any place for me to fit in. Mom and Aunt Jill were doing something awful looking with a dead turkey, Uncle Bill drove off someplace, and the two bigger Uffies

were watching cartoons on television in
the living room. They were both too little
to be interesting, and I didn't feel like
watching cartoons. This was a holiday,
and I felt like doing something
Thanksgivingy.

Then I remembered that I'd felt
sorry for Gramma Zee last night, the
way everybody bossed her around. I
went looking for her to see if I could do
something to make her happy.

She was in her tiny little bedroom
behind the dining room, sitting in a
rocking chair by the window and looking out at a snowy field.

"Hi, Gramma Zee. Do you want
company?"

"Might as well," she said through
her flopping lips. "Nothing good on television, and they won't let me go
outside."

"How come?" I plopped down on the
corner of her bed.

"Oh, who knows?" she griped.
"They think I'll catch pneumonia and

then they'll have to feel guilty when they inherit the farm. Bunch of nonsense. Fresh air is what keeps people alive. You been out this morning? What's the air like? Is it cold enough to make your eyes water?"

"Yeah, I went out, and no, it wasn't that cold. Just cold enough to make your nose run."

She nodded, understanding the fine points of weather reporting.

I said, "I went out to the barn. I was looking around in there and I found a sleigh, Gramma Zee. It was beautiful. I wanted to go for a ride in it, but . . ."

She nodded again. "No horse. I keep complaining about that myself, but they don't listen. They don't listen—they just say, 'Now now, Gramma, go to bed, drink your milk.' " She did a nasty imitation of how people talk to little kids and old people.

Then her eyes got happier and she swatted my knee. "That was my cutter you found, young Zelda. Not a sleigh—

a cutter. Built for speed. When I was a girl, I had a little horse named Lady, not much bigger than a pony she was, but fast! Lord, she was quick. She was half racehorse. I'd hitch her to that cutter just as soon as there was snow on the ground. Generally right around Thanksgiving time it was, too. We'd go at a nice quiet trot till we got around the corner of the barn where nobody could see, then, ZOWEE!" She yelled the *zowee* and half-raised up out of her chair, as if the reins were pulling at her hands.

Aunt Jill poked her head through the door and said, "You all right, Gramma?"

"Of course I'm all right, you twit."

"Remember your blood pressure," Aunt Jill said in a voice that sounded like she was patting Gramma on the head.

While that was going on, I was beginning to get one of my ideas. I sat and thought about it for a couple of minutes while Gramma grumbled and puffed her lips in and out.

Yes. It was a wonderful idea.

I bent over close to Gramma and whispered, "I'm going to take you for a ride in the cutter. You just give me about ten minutes to get things ready, and then you come out. I'll leave my orange sweatpants and my parka on the back porch. And my boots. All you have to do is wait till nobody's watching, sneak to the porch, and put on my stuff. If they see you out the window, they'll think it's me. Got it?"

It took a minute or so for the idea to settle into her head. Then she gave me a watery-eyed wink and said, "Got it. Now, where are you going to get a horse to pull the cutter?"

I patted her on the arm and said, "Just leave everything to me."

She gave me a Zelda-to-Zelda look and nodded.

◎

On the back porch I found a plaid jacket that was probably Aunt Jill's and put it on. The sleeves came over my hands, but that was okay. I squeezed into a pair of sweatpants from one of the Uffies and some big boots. I had to shuffle with my toes pointed up to keep them on.

The barn was empty when I got there. Whew. That was lucky. I looked out the big door at the back, and there were the cows all standing around looking bored.

"Okay," I said to them, "who wants to be a horse?"

They just looked at me.

I went back in the barn and found an ear of corn, in a little room full of ears of corn. I held it up over my head and said to the cows, "Okay, cows, here's what you get if you'll help me."

One great big cow started ambling toward me, and the rest of them followed her. I got her inside and slammed the door fast. One cow-horse was all I could handle.

While she was crunching the ear of corn, I found some ropes and tied one of them around her nose, then tied her to a post. This was going to be a piece of cake!

Next, I dragged the cutter out of the corner and got it up behind the cow. Real quick I dusted it off, then I went to work hitching up the cow-horse. I couldn't figure out how the horse harness went, and decided it probably wouldn't fit anyhow. Back to the ropes. I tied one around the cow-horse's neck and tied the other end to the cutter. Then I did the same thing again on the other side of the cow.

She was getting restless with all those ropes on her, so I got her some more corn and dumped it in front of her.

I shuffled over to the door and peeked out. Gramma Zee was coming! I could see my pink parka and orange sweatpants coming through the snow, lots slower than they usually traveled.

Just then Mom opened the back

door and yelled at her, "Zelda, you stay close to the house, now."

My parka hood nodded.

"And come in when you get cold."

The hood nodded again, and Gramma kept plodding toward the barn.

"And don't get into anything!"

The parka kept its head down but waved an arm.

"Have fun, dumpling," Mom called, and disappeared.

Whew.

Gramma Zee was out of breath by the time she got inside the barn. She had to lean on me and breathe for a couple of minutes. But she had a glowy look on her face, and her eyes were as sparkly as the snow outside.

"Fooled 'em," she said with a laugh in her voice. Then she saw the cutter and the cow-horse.

"Oh, my stars and garters," she breathed. "We are going for a ride!"

I shoved her up into the cutter, untied the cow and tossed the nose rope up to Gramma. Then I pushed and heaved till both of the big heavy doors had rolled back wide enough for us to drive through. Then, quickly, I ran and got in the cutter and took the rope. The reins . . . of the beautiful prancing horse. . . .

"Gee-up, Lady," Gramma yelled.

The cow turned her head around and stared at us.

I whomped her with the end of the rope on her big old hipbones. She slashed her tail back and forth.

Then, slowly, her front legs folded and she dropped to her knees, grunting. Her back end collapsed till she was clear down on the barn floor, curled up with her legs under her and her nose in what was left of the corn.

She was taking a nap!

I was so mad at her.

But when I looked at Gramma Zee, she was smiling a big soft smile and looking somewhere way far away.

"I remember one Thanksgiving when I was a girl, a little older than you. I must have been fourteen, fifteen that year. That was when I was pretty, as pretty as I ever got, anyhow. I was driving this very cutter, with Lady in the shafts."

Her hands came up to driving position, her feet splayed out against the front board, and I could almost see her remembering. I sat back beside her and pretended along with her.

It was way back then, that other Thanksgiving morning when Gramma Zee was young and beautiful and I wasn't even born yet. The sun was shining, and the snow was new and sparkly.

Gramma started talking.

"My cousins were down with the whooping cough that year, so our families couldn't have Thanksgiving dinner together like we usually did. So Ma had sent me over to their place with some sweet potato pie and jellied fruit she'd made extra for them.

"It was four miles over there, but with Lady out in front of me trotting along, and me driving faster than I was supposed to, it didn't take long at all. I delivered the food and started home, and along the road I met young Charlie Felsen out in his new cutter. Charlie was sweet on me. He wanted me to tie Lady on behind his cutter and ride with him, but I wouldn't. He wanted me to marry him was what he really wanted, but I hadn't made up my mind yet. Charlie was a nice boy, but he didn't have much spunk about him.

"We drove along side by side for a while, me trying to get him to race, and him being too polite to race against a girl. Then pretty soon along came Tom White from over in Boone Township. Tom was older and a little bit wild, and the handsomest thing I ever saw. He wanted me to marry him, too, but I wasn't sure if he'd be dependable enough.

"He drove up on the other side of

my rig and tipped his hat and wanted me to get in and ride with him. I kind of smiled and flirted with Tom and then with Charlie. Then I says to them, 'We'll have a race, from here to the covered bridge, and I'll marry the first one over the bridge.'

"What I didn't tell them was that I was in the race, too. I yelled 'Ready, set, GO!' and then I gave Lady a whomp with the reins and all three of us were off neck and neck down the road.

"There weren't six inches between our rigs. We sailed down that road hoping we wouldn't meet anybody coming the other direction. My runners hit Tom's and clanged and bounced off, and I almost fell out. I was standing up, just balancing against the wind and Lady's reins, my blood full of fire and my face full of wind.

"The road curved and started down a long, winding hill down to the river valley. My cutter leaned out on one runner and Lady slipped and skidded, but we stayed up and kept going. Down the hill, around the last bend, and into the straightaway.

"Up ahead I could see the covered bridge. It was only wide enough for one rig at a time, and there was a sharp turn just before the bridge. We were all three still running close together as we came up to the curve.

"Then Tom tried to swing wide to get around me. His cutter hit a bump and got off into deep snow at the edge of the road and slowed down just enough for me to pull over in front of him. Charlie and me went around the curve together and started up the slope onto the bridge. It looked like a good race, that last few jumps up into the bridge, but then Charlie pulled up and let me in ahead of him. Lady and I thundered across that bridge and won the race.

"Charlie and Tom come up to me and Charlie says, 'Tie Lady on behind my rig and ride with me, Zelda. This

means you marry me. I won the race.'
And I says, 'The heck you did, Charlie.
I won the race myself.'

"Well, Charlie cussed and grumbled
and tried to tell me he was just being a
gentleman, letting a lady cross the
bridge ahead of him. But I knew it
wasn't manners that made him pull
back. It was fear. I didn't want to marry
a coward."

"So you married Tom," I said.

"Nope. What drove Tom into the
ditch was carelessness and lack of good
sense. I didn't want that kind of husband, either. So I waited till a man came
along who was actually good enough for
me, and I married him. But that
Thanksgiving Day I was just being wild
and foolish and loving the whole snowy
world."

I said, "Did you spend some time in
the woodshed when you got home?"

She gave me a wink. "Most of the
afternoon. But it was worth it."

Just then the opened barn door was

filled with people chattering and waving their arms, Mom and Uncle Bill and Aunt Jill and all the little Uffies.

Mom yelled, "Zelda Marie Hammersmith! You are in big trouble now, young lady. Get down from there this very minute before you get hurt. I'm going to paddle you till my arm falls off!"

Uncle Bill lifted Gramma Zee down from the cutter and carried her off to the house like she was a baby, with Aunt Jill fluttering around chirping about pneumonia. Buffy and Duffy stared at the cow while Mom and I untied all the ropes and led her outside to the other cows. The Uffies turned and ran, though, when it looked like Mom was going to get down to the spanking part.

She took me by the shoulders and stared down at me in my big boots and huge jacket with the sleeves hanging over my hands. "Why did you do it, Zelda? Don't you know how dangerous that was, taking an eighty-nine-year-old woman out in this cold weather, putting her in a sled tied to a cow? If that cow had taken off running, you could have both been hurt. Killed, even. I'm going to have to spank you good and hard for this."

I nodded. She was right. I could see now—it had been a dumb and dangerous thing to do. Kind of like racing in a cutter with two boys who wanted to marry you.

"But we have to go to the woodshed," I said.

◎

The whole family sat at the big dining room table, with a glisteny-brown turkey at one end and Uffies all around.

I sat on a pillow.

Mom sat beside me, piling more food onto my plate than I could ever eat and trying to make up to me for the spanking. But I wasn't mad at her—not with Gramma Zee on my other side, throwing me warm looks and winks.

Before we started eating, Uncle Bill
made us stand up and hold hands while
he said a very long blessing. When he
got through talking to God, he said, "We
have a tradition in our family. At
Thanksgiving, we all go around the table and tell what we are the most thankful for this year. Buffy, you start."

Buffy screwed up her face and
thought. "I'm the most thankful for . . .
my friends. And my Julia doll. And my
pink dress with the—"

"Thank you," Uncle Bill inter-
rupted. "Duff?"

Duffy was too little or too dumb to
think of anything to be thankful for. Finally he looked around the table and
said, "Dessert."

"Fine," Uncle Bill translated.
"Duffer is thankful for all this bountiful
good food that comes from God's bountiful earth."

I didn't really think that was what
Duffy meant.

Aunt Jill shot me a glance and said,

"I'm thankful that we are all well and healthy, in spite of the unwise risks some of us take with other people's health and well-being."

Uncle Bill said, "I'm thankful today for this family and for the members of it who only visit occasionally." He shot that last part in my direction.

It was my turn. I said I was thankful for my friends and family. It came out sounding dumb, and it wasn't exactly what I meant. What I meant was Gramma Zee, who was more like me than anybody I ever knew, even without teeth and hair. It was like our minds were twins.

Mom looked down at me before she took her turn, and then she looked past me at Gramma Zee, who still had a glowy face, and I could see Mom beginning to understand things.

She put her arm around me and said in a clear voice, "I'm most thankful for a loving and giving daughter who isn't afraid to take chances and have

adventures, and who will have a trea-
sure of happy memories by the time
she's an old lady."

The Uffies started to grab for the
food, but Gramma Zee said, "Don't forget me. I get a turn here, too. I am most
thankful for . . . the best sleigh ride of
my whole life."

And she gave me a hug.

◎

As we drove home that night, Mom held
my feet in her lap and sang, " 'Over the
river and through the woods, to Grandmother's house we go. . . .' "

And I muttered in a sleepy voice,
" 'The cow knows the way to carry the
sleigh. . . .' "

3. Here Comes Zelda Claus

I have grave doubts about this, Zelda," Mom said.

We'd been having this argument all the way over to the shopping mall, and now we were standing just inside the mall door still having it.

"I'm big enough to shop alone," I insisted. "I know my way around this mall better than anybody. I won't get lost. And we both have to shop alone, for presents."

It was a week before Christmas, and I had forty dollars Mom had given me. I had to get Christmas presents for Mrs. Birdsall, my sitter, and for Mrs. Green, my teacher, and one to send to Daddy, who was in Nashville trying to become a singing star. And most important, I had to get something wonderful for Mom.

And even more important than that, Mom had to get something wonderful for me. So we both needed to go and shop alone. How could she buy my wonderful presents with me there watching?

She looked down at me, with doubt all over her face. "You won't speak to strange men, will you?"

I thought about that. "How can I tell how strange they are if I don't talk to them?"

"You don't talk to anybody, Zelda Marie, you got that? Only to store clerks. Let's see, it's quarter till six now.

Meet me by the fountain at seven o'clock. You know where the fountain is."

I nodded hard and fast. She was going to let me shop alone!

"And Zelda"—she gave me her crabbiest look—"do NOT get into any trouble of any kind."

"Trouble?" I asked.

"Trouble," she said.

"Me?" I asked.

"You," she said.

I promised, and she sighed and looked like she might change her mind any minute, so I gave her a smooch and ran off.

The shopping mall was like a dream world. I went crazy. Everything was sparkly and snowy and jingly, and Christmas music came down from the sky. The mall was shaped like a big cross, with stores along all four arms, and a big fountain in the middle where the four arms met.

Sometimes they had antique shows

or art shows or flea markets around the fountain, but tonight it was all Santa stuff. There was a Santa in a big chair with little kids getting their pictures taken talking to him. Behind him was his house, tall and skinny and made out of fake gingerbread, with candy and frosting all over it. There was a North Pole like a giant candy cane, and a sleigh with mechanical reindeer that nodded their heads and pawed the ground. Rudolph's nose flashed on and off. It was a red light bulb, I could tell. There was fake snow all over Santa's lawn, and a man no taller than me, dressed like an elf.

I wished I had more time to stand and watch, but I didn't. I ran to the Woolworth's and bought some country music tapes for Daddy and some pretty white mittens for Mrs. Birdsall and a pen in a real wood box for Mrs. Green. Those were the easy ones.

Now for Mom. I only had fourteen dollars left, and her present would have to be the best thing in the whole mall.

I started down the row of stores, looking in all the windows, and pretty soon I saw it!

It was in the window of a store called Nights of Fantasy, and it was the most beautiful nightgown I'd ever seen. It was black with red lace and purple ribbons, and you could see right through it. It would be very cool in summer.

Mom would look beautiful in it. Her usual nightgown was a shirt with stripes and a number across the chest, like a jail prisoner.

The big trouble with the beautiful black nightgown was the price: $69.95. I ran in the store and asked the lady if she could let me have it for $14.00, but she just snorted.

I kept looking in more store windows, but there was nothing else I wanted to give Mom. That black and red and purple nightgown was just perfect for her.

I stopped walking so I could think better. There was another Santa standing there, the kind that rings bells and wants people to put money into a big pot that says *Salvation Army* on it.

While I stood there, three people went by and put money into this pot. *Boy*, I thought, *I wish I could get money that easily*. Mom would have her nightgown in no time.

The man in the Santa suit looked at his watch, scooped all the money out of the pot, and set his bell down inside the pot. Then he walked off toward the men's rest room. I followed him, for no special reason.

I went in the ladies' room, and as I was coming out, the Santa man came out of the men's room dressed in regular clothes.

Aha, I thought, *he left the Santa suit in the rest room.*

As I watched, he went across the way and into the Burger King.

It was then that I got my Plan.

◎

I had to go into the men's room to get the suit. But I wasn't allowed in the men's room. But I had to go in there. So I did.

I ran in when nobody was watching. There was no one inside. Whew. Over against one wall was a coatrack, and hanging on the rack was the Santa suit, with cap and beard, and tall black boots standing under it.

The door opened and a man started to come in. He saw me, paused, looked confused, backed out again and read the *Men* on the door. Then he looked back at me, still confused.

I grabbed the Santa suit, hanger and boots and all, and said "Dry cleaners" as I ran past him out into the hall.

Quick thinking, Zelda, I told myself. But there was no time for congratulations. I'd have to work fast if I was going to get more than fifty-five dollars and get the suit back to the men's room before the Santa guy finished his supper break.

I ran into the ladies' room and started pulling on the suit. I couldn't see anybody, but I could hear a lady in one of the stalls, saying, "Hurry up, we haven't got all day." A little kid's voice said, "I don't want to go." And the mommy said, "You have to."

I pulled on the red pants. Of course they were hugely too big for me and kept falling down. I flop-flopped into an empty stall and pulled off wads and wads of toilet paper and stuffed them around my middle to make a Santa belly.

Then I stepped into the high black boots. I had to hang onto the sink and pick my legs way up, because the boots came all the way to the tops of my legs. I couldn't bend my knees at all.

The red jacket with the white cotton fluffs around the edges was the easy part. The sleeves came way off the ends of my arms, but I just pushed them up.

The beard had two hooks on it to hook over my ears, but it was so big that it kept coming unhooked off of my right ear and hanging crooked off my left ear.

And then I put the cap on—the red Santa cap with white fluffs around it. It slipped clear down over my face. I couldn't see a thing except for my own cheeks and nose and crooked beard. Finally I fixed the beard problem by sticking my nose through the mouth hole so that the whole beard was hanging from my nose. That meant the mustache part was up in front of my eyes, though.

Time was passing. No time for fiddling around with details. I shoved up the cap, pulled down the beard, grabbed my bag of presents, and shuffle-hopped the big black boots out of the rest room and across the way to the Salvation Army kettle.

I reached inside, got the bell, and started ringing it. My cap slipped down over my face again.

Somebody came by and put some

money into the kettle. I couldn't see them but I heard a woman trying not to laugh. "That's the funniest looking Santa I've ever seen."

"I'm one of his helpers," I bellowed from under my cap. The beard came unhooked from nose and ear.

More money clanked into the kettle. Yay, hurray! I rang like crazy and yelled "Thank you, bless you, Merry Christmas" all over the place.

I began hearing more sputtering and whispering and giggling, as more and more people slowed down, walking past me. But that was fine with me. Money clanked into the kettle, and I thought I even heard a few dollar bills.

I pushed up my cap for a quick peek. It looked like lots of money down in there. Another ten minutes and that black and red and purple nightgown was in the bag.

Then I looked down the way, and there was Mom, coming along looking in store windows.

Help.

As far as my boots would let me bend, I got down behind the kettle, like I was fishing for something I dropped. I tried to peek around to see if she was still coming, but I was having too much trouble with the boots that kept my legs straight, the toilet paper that kept shifting around my middle, and the cap and beard that were either slipping down or poking up in front of my eyes.

Then I saw Mom's boots turn and go into a store. I'd have to hurry up and get the rest of the money before she came out. Luckily, it was a music store—she always spent lots of time looking at cassettes when she went into music stores.

As I straightened up I almost fell into the kettle because I couldn't bend my knees. Ring, ring, ring. "Ho ho ho, Merry Christmas. Thank you. Bless you. Merry Christmas."

I rang faster and faster, hoping people would drop money in faster and faster, too. It was time to get the suit back to the men's room, time to buy the black nightgown and meet Mom at the fountain.

I was just giving the old bell one last big chorus of rings when I looked down the way and saw . . .

Trouble. Big trouble.

It was the Santa man and another man in a security guard uniform. They were three stores away, but they'd stopped and they were staring and pointing.

At me.

◎

Did you ever try run for your life in boots that came clear up your legs and kept slipping off your feet with your beard swinging from one ear and your cap clear down over your face? With toilet paper streaming out behind you like a kite's tail?

Well, don't ever try it.

I grabbed my sack of presents and

took off running, with the bell still in my hands. It was like running on stilts. I fell down and the boots started coming off. I kicked free from them and ripped off my cap. Then I could really run.

Up the mall I bolted, ringing my bell to get people out of my way. The beard was flapping in the wind. The toilet paper was almost all unrolled by now and streaming out behind me.

The men were gaining on me.

Up ahead was the main Santa, with the mechanical reindeer and the gingerbread house beside the fountain.

I ducked around the reindeer, snagged my beard and left it hanging from Rudolph's nose. Over the low picket fence I leapt, right into the arms of the little man in the elf suit.

"Go to the end of the line if you want to talk to Santy," he said in a gravelly voice.

I bopped him with my bag of presents. "I AM Santy," I yelled at him. "Let go of me."

"Ho ho ho," said the Santa on the chair. "Are we having a little disturbance down there, Misha the Elf?"

"I got it under control," the elf snarled back. "Keep your fuzz on."

"Ho ho ho," the Santa said. "Santa's elves shouldn't get testy. Elves who mouth off to Santa find themselves back in the unemployment office, don't they?"

I didn't have time for this. My own Santa man and the security guard were gaining on me.

Misha the Elf had me by the jacket, but that was no problem. I dropped bell and packages, hunched out of the jacket and left him holding it. I bolted around him and into the Santa house.

I should have known better. It was just an empty square about the size of a bathroom, but very tall. It had boards across the walls where it was nailed together.

If I got high enough, maybe they wouldn't see me when they looked inside. They'd think I went out another way—through the window, maybe.

I grabbed a board and started climbing. Up I went, and up some more. It was exciting!

I got clear up by the top and was hanging there waiting for danger to pass when all of a sudden I heard a ripping sound, like nails pulling out of boards.

The wall I was hanging onto started to sway and twist.

Oh, no.

Help.

Suddenly the wall and I were falling forward. Crash, splash! Water was all over me. Thin boards fell through the air.

The gingerbread house came down around me.

I sat in the shallow water of the fountain and bawled.

People were screaming and running around, fishing me out of the water.

"Are you all right? Are you hurt?" they kept asking me.

I wished I was hurt. If I was hurt, everybody would feel sorry for me instead of mad.

My Santa man and the security guard hoisted me by the elbows and let me drip between them. They looked down at me, and I looked over at the gingerbread Santa's house.

One wall was still more or less standing up, but it was wavering. The other three walls and the roof were all in the fountain. The picture-taking Santa and Misha the Crabby Elf were staring at me and at their house like they couldn't believe it.

Well, it wasn't that good of a house. It didn't have furniture or anything inside it. I didn't believe that Santa guy lived in it at all, even during Christmas-shopping season when he was on duty.

My Santa guy started shaking me by the arm and saying, "What did you steal my suit for, you little juvenile delinquent?"

I gave him a haughty look. "I'm not supposed to speak to strange men."

"All right, sis," the security guard said. "You'll have to come along with me to the office."

"Am I under arrest?" I said in a tiny voice. I supposed this would qualify as getting into trouble, in Mom's opinion.

Then I looked up and saw Mom standing and staring from the other side of Rudolph, who was still bobbing his head and blinking his nose, my beard swinging from it.

"Zelda Marie Hammersmith," she said with a weary sigh. And I knew I'd done it again.

◎

We all gathered up stuff—the boots and beard and jacket and cap, and my bag of presents. Then we went down a long hallway to the security guard's office. They got the whole story out of me there.

"It was $69.95," I wailed. "And it was so beautiful, Mom. You can see right through it, and it was so shiny and black, with all that red lace and purple ribbons all over it. It was lots more beautiful than your jail nightshirt."

"Jail nightshirt?" the guard said, looking at Mom with new suspicion. "You've done time, have you?"

But Mom was ignoring him and staring into my face. She held me by the shoulders so I had to look at her.

"What you did was wrong, Zelda Marie. You stole this man's costume. You took money from people under false pretenses."

"And I went in the men's rest room," I added in a tiny voice.

"That, too. And you broke the Santa house."

I started to bawl again.

The Santa man left the room suddenly and came back with a wad of money in his hand. It was my money from the kettle. "No harm done there," he said in a grudging voice. "Actually, she collected more in half an hour than I'd gotten all afternoon."

"Do I get to keep it?" I asked, suddenly cheerful.

"NO!" they all yelled at me.

Mom said, "The people who gave that money thought they were giving it to help poor people."

The guard said, "Not to buy sexy lingerie for women with prison records and dubious professions."

"Look, buster," Mom turned on him, "I am a sausage stuffer at a packing plant and I've never been in jail in my life, so just shut up. Okay. Zelda. This man has his Santa suit back—no harm done there. He has the money you collected, so no harm done there."

"What about the gingerbread house?" the guard said, glaring at us.

Mom thought about that. "Zelda broke it, and Zelda will help rebuild it."

The guard thought about that for about half a second. "No thanks. I don't want that kid anywhere near any of the displays. Ever again. Never. Ever. Just get her out of here."

As we started out the door, I said to the Santa guy, "If you have trouble keeping your beard on, stick your nose through the mouth hole."

"Get out of here," he bellowed. I didn't think Santa guys were ever supposed to yell at little kids.

◎

Mom and I had a wonderful Christmas morning. I stayed in my own bed till way after five. Then I couldn't stand it any longer and went and jumped in with her and she hugged me and blew in my hair and did spider-walks up my belly with her fingers.

Then we got up and turned on Christmas music on TV, and I had to wait while she made coffee for herself and poured orange juice for me.

Our tree was just a little one on the table in front of the window, because

trailers don't have very big living rooms.
But it was a beautiful tree. We'd gone
out to the tree farm and cut it down
ourselves, and all our friends came over
the night we decorated it—Cindy and
Kimberley and Mrs. Birdsall.

Now it looked so beautiful with all
the packages around the bottom that I
almost cried, knowing the packages
would all be opened ten minutes from
now.

I already knew my presents
wouldn't be very expensive because sausage stuffers don't make lots of money,
but that was okay. Mom always thought
a lot about everything she gave me, so
it was always good stuff that was just
right for me.

I ripped in and opened everything,
and loved everything. Then I sat back
and watched while Mom opened my
present to her.

As she unfolded it and lifted it from
the box, she got a big smile all over her
face. Love was in her eyes as she held

the present up to her front, and looked at me over it.

"It's the most beautiful nightgown I ever had," she said. She ran her hands lovingly over the fourteen-dollar night-shirt with prison stripes and a number across it.

4. Be My Valentine, Zelda Hammersmith

You wouldn't think anybody could get into trouble at a school Valentine's Day party, would you? Not even me.

Well, you'd be WRONG.

Valentine's Day was going to be on Friday. On Wednesday, Mrs. Green told us about our party.

"You boys and girls will decorate a big box tomorrow," she said. "And you can put valentines in the box for all your friends in class. Then on Friday, we'll open the box and deliver the valentines, and we'll have a special little treat."

I knew all about Mrs. Green's Valentine's Day parties. The big brother of my best friend, Kimberley, had had Mrs. Green, and he said her Valentine's Day parties were the boringest he'd ever seen. All you got for refreshments were those little hard candy hearts that say *Cutie* and *Sweetie Pie* on them.

Still, a boring party was better than doing arithmetic on a Friday afternoon. I was fairly excited about it.

At lunch that day, we talked about the party—Kimberley and me and Brinda Burgess, who is in a different fourth-grade room. She has Miss Meadows, the lucky stiff. Miss Meadows is young and happy and jokey and wears big red sweaters. She'd be more fun to look at all day than Mrs. Green, who is sort of huge and old and dark-dressy.

Brinda said, "For our Valentine's Day party we're going to have a cookie-decorating contest, and a prettiest-valentine contest, and all of us kids are going together to buy Miss Meadows a big heart-shaped box of chocolate candy."

"Wow," I breathed. I was so jealous of their Valentine's Day party. I was jealous of them having a teacher they loved so much that they'd buy her a box of candy.

I thought about our class buying candy for Mrs. Green. It wouldn't work. Nobody would want to. Nobody liked her that much.

That thought made me so sad I quit eating my little square of orange Jell-O and my triangle of buttered bread.

Probably Mrs. Green knew nobody loved her. Probably after our parties Miss Meadows would take her candy box to the teachers' lounge and show it off, and Mrs. Green would feel awful because her kids didn't love her enough to give her a special valentine.

Then I thought, probably people who never get valentines NEED them a whole lot more than people who get them all the time.

I chewed slower and slower. I was beginning to form a Plan.

◎

I could hardly wait for Mom to get home from work that night so I could tell her about it and get her to help. As soon as her car drove up in front of our trailer, I ran home from next door, where Mrs. Birdsall takes care of me after school.

I crashed into Mom by the front door and gave her a giant hug. I get smothered in her stomach when I do that, but it's worth it.

"Hi, dumpling," she said as she danced me through the door. "Did you have a good day at school? What did you learn? Don't talk to me till I get unwound."

That meant I had to wait till she got out of her work jeans and into her home jeans and her *Keep on Truckin'* sweat-shirt and her sloppy slippers. Then I had to wait till she got her can of Moun-tain Dew opened, till she sank down in her chair and let her hands hang down for a while. She had to do that every day because she got so tired running her sausage-stuffing machine at work.

FINALLY she was ready for me.

"We're going to have a big surprise for Mrs. Green for Valentine's Day," I said. "You know the big box that the valentines go in? Well, one of the boys is going to dress up like Cupid, with a bow and arrow and diaper and everything. And when Mrs. Green opens the box to pass out our valentines, he's going to jump out and pretend to shoot love at her with his bow and arrow, and then he's going to sing her a special song. I'm going to write the song myself."

Mom looked at me with her eyebrows up. "Uh . . . huh. Whose idea was all this, Zelda?"

"Mine," I grinned all over my face.

"I thought so. It sounds like a lovely surprise, dumpling. That was very thoughtful of you. Does Mrs. Green have any history of heart attacks, do you know?"

Sometimes Mom asks strange questions. I let it pass.

"Mrs. Green asked for somebody to bring a big cardboard box tomorrow so we can decorate it for the valentine mailbox. I said I'd bring it. Would you help me find one?"

She gave it some thought. "As I was driving in just now I saw the Gundersons unloading a big box. It looked like maybe a television set. You could check with them. Otherwise we can take a ride over to the grocery store after supper. They've always got boxes."

I bounced out the door and ran all the way down to the end of the trailer park to the Gundersons' trailer before I realized I didn't have my parka on.

The box was sitting empty in their garage and it was perfect. It said *Motorola 19" Console* on the side, but we'd cover that up with our decorations. I got in it and scrunched down to make sure it was big enough, and it was. And Mrs. Gunderson said I was welcome to it.

I hopped all the way home with the box over my head, so all I could see was my feet and the sidewalk, one square at a time.

I couldn't talk to Mom while we ate supper because she was on the phone talking to her friend Cindy the whole time. She'd eat while Cindy was talking, then she'd talk a while so Cindy could eat her supper. Cindy had Darrell and her ex-husband both expecting to take her out on Valentine's Day night, so she needed quite a bit of advice from Mom.

Finally Mom hung up and got back to important things. Me.

"I need something for Cupid's diaper," I said. "How come Cupid always wears a diaper, anyhow?"

Mom shrugged. "You may not believe this," she said, "but until this moment I have never asked myself that burning question. Let's see, what could you use? A dish towel?"

We got up from the table and pawed through the dish towels. Most of them were a dingy grayish color from being old and used, or else they had roosters or pigs on them. But we finally found one that was white on one side. I tried it on myself, over my jeans, and it was just right for a diaper. It had roosters on the inside, but that didn't matter.

"Who is going to be Cupid?" Mom asked.

"Well . . . I don't know yet. It has to be a boy, because Cupid is a boy and we have to do this right. But at recess I asked all the boys in the class and none of them really wanted to do it very badly."

"Never in a million years" was what they had said. The polite ones. What the other ones said I'd get paddled for if I repeated it. But I figured I'd talk somebody into the job between now and Friday.

All I had left to do was to write the song. I worked on it till bedtime, and then I sang it for Mom. She thought it was wonderful. So did I. It was to the tune of "Jingle Bells," and it went:

> Mrs. Green, Mrs. Green,
> Be our valentine,
> Because we
> All agree,
> You are nice and kind.

◎

The next morning at school, Gerald came up to me at my locker while I was still getting off my boots and parka.

Gerald is the kind of boy you get suspicious of any time he comes up to you. Especially if he's all smiley and friendly, like he was now. He was always luring kids behind the puppet theater in the library, telling them he had a present for them. He'd hold his fists like there was something good in his hands, and then when you got close enough, he'd grab you and twist the skin on your arm and give you an arm burn.

I hated him.

He was littler than me, and his hair stuck out in chopped-off spikes all over his head, and he always had a finger up his nose. Nobody liked him. Last year on Valentine's Day he only got three valentines. And we were all supposed to give to everybody in the class.

Gerald is an awful hard person to give a valentine to.

So when he came up to me with that smile on his face, I naturally got a good hold on my geography book in case I needed to bonk him. My geography book is the heaviest book I've got, with all those maps and rainfall charts.

Gerald gave me the kind of smile he used to lure his victims behind the puppet stage. "Hey, Zelda, I decided I'd be the Cupid."

I stared at him suspiciously. "You have to wear a diaper, and carry a little play bow and arrow, and jump out of the box and sing a song."

"I know. I'll do it."

I looked into his shifty little eyes and I didn't trust him. Not for one minute. "I'll think about it and I'll let you know at lunch," I told him.

When I dragged the Motorola box into our room and showed it to Mrs. Green, she put her hands up to her throat like she was choking. "My goodness, Zelda. That's much too big a box. We don't want a box that big. Couldn't you find one about half that size?"

I tried to keep the twinkle out of my eyes. She didn't know the secret of why we needed a big box. I shook my head and looked down at the Motorola box.

Mrs. Green just sighed and gave me a look, making room for the box on the table beside her desk.

During the morning, while we were all moving around the room working on the decorations for the box, I whispered to every boy in the class, "Please be the Cupid. If you don't, Gerald is going to."

They all turned me down—again.

By lunchtime it was clear that I was stuck with Gerald for my Cupid, like it or not.

◎

Valentine's Day morning. Finally. I was so excited, I could hardly eat my breakfast.

I gave Mom her super-duper valentine that I had made at school, with real lace around the edge and lettering with hardly any smudges.

She gave me a giant hug and kiss, and a new top to wear with my red slacks. It was white, with big puffy sleeves and red hearts all across the front with *Love ya* written in each heart. I put it on. It was perfect for a Valentine's Day party.

When I got to school, I took all the valentines I'd made for everybody and stuffed them through the slot in the Motorola box, just like everybody else was doing.

The box was beautiful. Mrs. Green

had even quit complaining about how big it was. It was all covered with white crepe paper with red twisty streamers looping from the corners, and big red letters and hearts that we'd cut from construction paper. The letters said *Valentine Mailbox.*

The party wasn't till two o'clock, so we had to keep our shirts on all day. It was hard.

At lunchtime I went into the principal's office and let him in on the secret, and he promised to do his part. He is very nice, for a principal.

It took forever, but finally two o'clock got there.

Mrs. Green closed the book she'd been reading from, checked her watch, and said, "All right, boys and girls. Time for valentines."

I got worried. Where was . . . ah. Just in time.

The principal's voice came out of the intercom up by the ceiling. "Mrs.

Green, could you come to the office for a moment, please?"

Whew.

"You boys and girls stay in your seats and be very quiet. I'll be right back. Kimberley, you are in charge."

We sat like statues till the door closed behind her. Then we all shot out of our seats. Our lockers are all across the back of the room. I ran to mine and got out the dish towel and the big safety pins Mom gave me.

"Okay, Gerald," I hissed. "Take off your pants and shirt. Get your diaper on, quick. Where's your bow and arrow?"

He skinned off his shirt, but he wouldn't take his jeans off. He grabbed hold of them and glared at the three boys who were trying to pull them off.

"I'm not taking my jeans off," he snarled. "I'll put the dish towel on over them, but I'm not taking them off."

We didn't have time to fight him. Mrs. Green could be back at any second. I glared at him as hard as I could, but finally I gave in and started wrapping the dish towel around him. I never wanted to stick a safety pin into anybody so much in my whole life.

The dish towel looked stupid over his jeans. Especially with his little skinny bare chest on top.

"Get your bow and arrow," I hissed. "Hurry up."

He reached into his locker and brought out . . . a squirt gun.

"I didn't have a bow and arrow," he said, smiling his nasty smile.

"You can't use a squirt gun," I yelled. "Cupid didn't have a squirt gun to shoot love at people, you jerk. What kind of Cupid would use a squirt gun?"

He just shrugged and grinned.

At noon, I'd given him a copy of the song and told him to learn it by heart. "Did you learn the song?" I asked him now. He gave me a funny look, but nodded.

Kimberley, who was watching at the door, said, "Here she comes. Hurry up."

No more time! We hustled Gerald up to the front of the room, onto the table, into the box. I bonked him on the back of his head, harder than I needed to, to get him scrunched down. We closed the box lid and got into our seats just as the door opened and Mrs. Green came in.

She looked at us all, like she knew we'd been out of our seats, but she didn't say anything, and she didn't notice Gerald's empty seat.

"All right, boys and girls. Time for our valentines. Who wants to be the postman and deliver them?"

We looked at each other.

"Why don't you be the postman?" I said. I couldn't keep the twinkle off of my face anymore. I could hardly wait for her to open the box and get her very own

singing valentine from a real live Cupid.
I could hardly wait for her to go to the
teachers' lounge and brag about the
wonderful surprise her class had given
her.

She looked around the room at all
our bright smiling faces. "All right, if
you want me to," she said, and almost
smiled herself. It was working already!

She reached for the top of the box
to open it, but it flew open itself, and
up popped Gerald, just like he was supposed to.

Only it was hard to tell that he was
Cupid, with that dumb gun in his hand
and his dish towel slipping halfway
down his legs. While Mrs. Green
grabbed at her throat in surprise, he
began to sing.

"Mrs. Green, Mrs. Green,
Don't be our valentine.
Zelda Hammersmith thinks
Your feet stinks,
And your face is like an orange rind."

Then he began shooting water at everybody and tromping up and down on all those beautiful valentines in the bottom of the box.

Mrs. Green stared at him, and then at me.

I started to bawl.

Kimberley started to bawl, too, because she was my best friend. Then Angela and Tina and all three of the Jennifers started crying, and then the boys started in laughing nervously and pretty soon the whole class was laughing, crying, or both together.

I looked at Gerald standing up there in the Motorola box with his dish towel hanging half off and his gun dripping water onto the valentines, a mean stupid look on his mean stupid face.

I looked at Mrs. Green, who looked like she was about to bawl herself, or else choke.

Then I couldn't see them anymore because I was bawling so hard.

That was when the principal opened our door to poke his head in and see if Mrs. Green was enjoying her surprise valentine.

◎

Finally we got it all straightened out. We took what were left of the valentines out of the box and passed them around, and got the dish towel off of Gerald just before he left for a trip to the office with the principal.

Then Mrs. Green said, "Zelda, perhaps you'd like to take over Gerald's role."

So I put the diaper on over my red slacks and tied a string onto Mrs. Green's yardstick to make a bow, then got into the box.

"All right, Zelda, I'm ready to be surprised," Mrs. Green called.

Majestically I rose, bowed, pretended to shoot love at everybody with my bow, and sang.

"Mrs. Green, Mrs. Green,
Be our valentine.
Because we
All agree
You are nice and kind."

You're not going to believe this. I almost didn't believe it myself. When Mrs. Green lifted me out of the box and set me down, she gave me an actual HUG.

5. Zelda and the Golden Egg

I sat on the school bus with an armload of happiness on my lap. It was a cage, and inside the cage was Bugs, our class rabbit.

The smile all over my face was because I was the big winner. Mrs. Green had drawn names of everybody in our class to see who would get to take Bugs home for the Easter weekend, and Zelda Hammersmith had been IT!

We'd only had Bugs in our room for three weeks. Mrs. Green wasn't very big on having animals in her classroom.

She said they took our attention away from our books. Of course they did. Who wouldn't rather watch a darling white bunny with black ears and a black nose than an arithmetic book?

But one of the sixth-grade rooms had more rabbits than they had space for, so our room got one. Every Friday afternoon we had a drawing to see who would take Bugs home for the weekend so he wouldn't starve or die of a dirty cage. I wanted to win so bad it was hard to keep from whining when I didn't.

Finally I won! And the best part was, it was the start of Easter vacation, so I'd have Bugs for four whole days, not just two.

My best friend, Kimberley, had to sit clear over on the edge of the seat so the cage wouldn't touch her. She's so clean and neat she never gets any fun out of life except for being clean and neat. Personally, I'd rather have a rabbit on my lap, but that's just the way Kimberley is.

She said, "I wonder what Mr. Batman will think about having a rabbit next door. It might hurt his feelings."

I'd never thought of that. It would be awful if Mr. Batman got his feelings hurt, because he was my guinea pig and my best friend. Besides Mom and Kimberley. He lived in a cage on the floor by my bed, but just between you and me, he spent a lot of time on my pillow and under the covers. He'd run his whiskery nose over my face and make me giggle myself silly.

I opened the lid of the cardboard box that Bugs's cage was in and looked at him. He had his ears back and his eyes closed, like he was afraid something bad was about to happen to him. I wished I could tell him I loved him and that I'd take care of him.

"Mr. Batman will be glad to have company," I said firmly. "Bugs and Bats can talk nose-wiggle talk through their cages at each other. They'll be best friends."

Then I got a pain in my heart,

thinking about them being best friends without me. I wanted both of them to love me, not each other.

Life and love are two of the most complicated things there are, probably.

Kimberley's elbow started nudging at me, like she wanted me to notice something.

"What?" I said.

She just nudged again.

Then I saw the eye. It was looking through the crack between the two seats in front of me, and it was aimed right at the rabbit box.

When it shifted up toward me I said, "You want a look?"

The eye disappeared, and pretty soon a head came rising up over the back of the seat. It was a boy, a new one. I'd seen him getting on the bus that morning but I didn't know who he was.

He looked little and young and kind of dirty.

"Who are you?" I said.

He just stared at me.

"You want to see my rabbit?" I asked him.

His eyes got kind of hungry, and he nodded his head.

I folded back the box top and tipped it so he could look in. Bugs had to scramble to keep from sliding. The kid leaned way out over the back of the seat and hung there, staring down at Bugs.

The bus driver bellowed, "Down in your seat."

The kid slithered down and disappeared like a snake going into its hole.

We were getting close to Perfect Paradise, the trailer park where Kimberley and I live.

"Are you coming over tomorrow?" I asked her.

"I can't. We have to go to Uncle Jim's."

We looked at each other and sighed. One of the worst parts about being a kid is having to go to visit relatives, just because your mother wants to. Half the time there's nothing to do when you get there. The old people just sit around the kitchen table drinking boring coffee and talking about football teams or politics.

The bus stopped at our corner. The new kid jumped off in front of Kimberley and me and took off running. Kimberley helped me get the cage box down the bus steps, and helped me carry it toward home.

"You're going to the Easter Egg Hunt, aren't you?" she said.

"Of course. That's the best part of Easter. And I'm going to win it this year."

"Oh, Zelda, you're always saying things like that. You're always bragging what you're going to do and you never do it. You always mess things up some way."

I had to put Bugs down on the sidewalk, I got so mad at that. "I do not! I do too! I won the costume contest at the Halloween party," I yelled at her. "I made up a better costume than your stupid old butterfly."

"A bat," she spat. "And then you messed it up and almost killed yourself and broke the armory building. They only gave you the prize because you messed up in such a spectacular way."

"Ha," I said. It was all I could think of. "Ha to you, Kimberley Curtiss."

"Ha right back at you. Wait till the Easter Egg hunt. See who's saying 'ha' then."

"Okay." I gave her a glinting look. I love a challenge.

Every year, on Easter afternoon, the trailer park residents' committee puts on an Easter egg hunt for the kids in the neighborhood. The adults go out in the field behind the trailer park and hide a bunch of eggs in the long grass, and then give us all baskets and turn us loose. They have prizes for who can find the most green eggs or pink ones or whatever, and then there is a grand prize. There is one golden egg, and whoever finds that one gets money. It's the hardest one to find. Usually Kimberley's big brother, Kirk, finds it.

But this year I felt lucky. After all, I'd only had one chance in twenty-eight of winning the drawing for Bugs. And I'd won! So that meant this year I was getting the golden egg.

So ha to Kimberley.

Double ha.

◎

Mr. Batman didn't seem very thrilled about his new friend. He just sat in the far corner of his cage and stared at Bugs and kind of shivered.

Mom wasn't very thrilled either, but she didn't get all hunched and shivery— she just said it was my responsibility and not to let the rabbit out of the cage.

When I took Mr. Batman under the covers with me, he didn't run his whiskery nose over my face and make me giggle myself silly like he usually did. I told him and told him that Bugs was just visiting and that I loved Mr. Batman more than anybody in the world. But I don't think he believed me. He just went clear down by my feet under the covers and curled up there.

I kissed him on his whiskery nose when I finally put him back in his cage. He didn't move. He was really taking this hard. I took Bugs out for a minute because I had to kiss his nose good night too, and I had to explain that Mr. Batman was just jealous. I didn't want Bugs to get his feelings hurt.

The next morning I woke up thinking that probably Mr. Batman would be back to normal and we could play all day. I rolled over and looked down into his cage.

He was lying on his side with his feet sticking out kind of stiff. I got scared before I even realized what I was scared of.

And then I knew. I knew Mr. Batman was dead. I opened my mouth to yell for Mom, but I couldn't get it out.

So I ran and dragged her out of bed and made her follow my pointing finger because I had tears all over my face.

She came running, and took a close look at him. Then she wrapped me up in a big smothering hug and it hurt because I knew what it meant.

"I'm sorry, dumpling."

"But I did everything I was supposed to," I wailed. "I gave him his food every day and I never let his water dish get empty and I cleaned his cage just like I was supposed to."

"Yes, you did, dumpling. You took wonderful care of him." She stroked my hair.

"Then why did he die?" I was miserable.

She held me out by the shoulders then, and looked me in the face. "Zelda, everything has to die sometime. We don't know how old Mr. Batman was. He probably just died of old age. You gave him a wonderful life while you had him. No guinea pig ever had a better life.

It wasn't your fault. Here, toot your snoot."

She handed me a Kleenex.

For a while we sat on the edge of the bed and rocked, and then she said in a faraway voice. "Funny. Today is Good Friday. That's the day Jesus died. Mr. Batman picked a good day."

I kept thinking about that all morning. I couldn't figure out why they called it Good Friday if that was the day Jesus died. Why didn't they call it Horrible Friday?

Then I thought, *Jesus died on Good Friday, but he came back to life again on Easter Sunday.*

Mr. Batman died on Good Friday too. So maybe . . .

After lunch, Mom said, "What are you going to do with the deceased, Zelda? You can't just leave him lying in there, dead."

"I'm waiting for him to arise," I said. "On Easter Sunday morning he might rise from the dead and be alive again."

She gave me the longest, saddest look she'd ever had on her face. "Zelda darling dumpling sweetie-toes, it doesn't work that way. Dead is dead."

"It worked for Jesus," I argued.

"Well, Mr. Batman is not Jesus!"

"Yes, but . . ."

"No *buts*. Much as it pains me to say it, Mr. Batman is dead as a doornail and you can't leave him on your bedroom floor."

I thought about it for a long time. "He could have a funeral," I said slowly. "Only if I bury him, he won't be able to rise on Easter morning."

"Jesus managed," Mom said.

◎

I started getting excited about the funeral. I still felt all sad and lumpy-throated about Mr. Batman being dead, but if it was only for three days, I could stand that. And I'd get to be the boss of the funeral since he was my guinea pig.

It couldn't be until tomorrow, because Kimberley was at her uncle's all day and I wanted Mr. Batman to have a big funeral with as many mourners as possible. But there was lots to do in the meantime.

I went through my whole bedroom looking for the best thing to wrap him in. Finally I decided on my favorite T-shirt. It had a row of Miss Piggies in ballet costumes toe-dancing across the front. Of course Mr. Batman was a guinea pig, not a pig pig, but it was as close as I could come.

Mom started to say that I couldn't waste a good T-shirt that way, but then she closed her mouth and just looked sad at me. She even gave me the perfect thing for his coffin. It was a baking pan, a dark blue one with little white specks. It was shaped kind of like a guinea pig coffin. The best part was that it wasn't an old pan that she wanted to throw away anyhow. It was a good one that she made meat loaf in. It still even had some of the label stuck on the lid from when she'd bought it.

She is a good old mom.

I laid the T-shirt in the pan so the Miss Piggies would show, and then I laid the deceased in it and covered him up to his chin with the end of the shirt. He looked just like he did when he slept on my pillow with me.

I wanted to put the coffin on top of the television, so mourners could come to call and look at him. But Mom said no, he might get knocked off and spilled. And she didn't like the idea of the kitchen counter at all.

So the deceased went to lie in state on my dresser. I even made my bed, in case mourners noticed.

I tried to play with Bugs for a while before supper, but he didn't seem to want to be played with. And besides, I thought Mr. Batman might get his feelings hurt.

After supper I worked on my speech

and decided what to wear for the funeral. Finally I went to bed and cried a little bit because I missed the whiskery nose.

◎

Right after breakfast I went all up and down the trailer park inviting everyone to come to the funeral. It was funny how many people already had other plans.

Mrs. Birdsall next door said, "I'd love to come, dear, but I expect I'll be having a sinus attack this afternoon. Where are you going to . . . uh . . . bury the rat?"

"He's not a rat," I yelled. "He's a guinea pig, and he's adorable, and he's going to come to life again tomorrow morning just like Jesus did."

She gave me a look down her long nose.

"I'm going to bury him behind the tool shed," I said after I'd simmered down.

"Oh, my dear, you can't do that. You're not allowed to bury pets or animals anywhere on the trailer park grounds. It's a rule."

I hated rules.

"Well then, I'll bury him in the field out back. The funeral is at one o'clock, so please come if your sinus isn't attacking you right then." I turned and marched off with a very stiff back. Mrs. Birdsall had that effect on me sometimes.

I went over to Kimberley's to tell her the sad news and get her to help with the funeral. Their trailer was the biggest one in the park, two whole trailers wide, with a great big living room and three bedrooms. She was in hers, reading a book.

"Mr. Batman died yesterday," I told her.

She looked interested, instead of sad like she was supposed to. "What did it die of?"

"He's a *he*, not an *it*. I've told you that a million times. I don't know what he died of. Mom said probably old age."

I started to tell her that I was pretty sure he was going to rise again tomorrow morning like Jesus, but I stopped myself in time. Kimberley could be kind of mean about laughing at things like that. And lots of times she was right, and that always made me furious.

She opened her book again like she wanted to get back to reading. "It probably died of rabies or some awful disease, and you're going to get it, too."

"He did not!"

I yelled so loud her brother, Kirk, stuck his head in the door to see what was up. He was twelve. I was more or less planning to marry him when I got old, but for now I didn't much like him. He was even more of a know-it-all than Kimberley, and he was almost as neat.

"My guinea pig died," I told him. "The funeral is this afternoon at one o'clock. Will you come and play your French horn? We need some music."

He had to think about that. Guinea pig funerals might be under his level of dignity, but on the other hand, he loved to play his French horn and hardly anyone ever asked him to.

"Okay, I'll come," he said finally. "Got nothing else to do."

"Will you come?" I poked Kimberley, who couldn't seem to quit reading. She was reading *A Very Young Dancer*, which she'd already read four thousand times.

"I don't know," she said. "I don't much want to."

"Yes, but you're my best friend. This is part of your job. If you had something that you loved and it died, I'd come to the funeral, wouldn't I?"

She couldn't get around that one.

"Well, okay. Are you going to serve refreshments?"

"If I have to."

"Get your mom to make one of those

marble cakes with the cherry and chocolate cake all swirled in together."

"Is that the price of your friendship?" I asked sadly.

"Yes. Cake and pop."

I sighed.

◎

Each trailer in the park has a shade tree in front of it. I stood under our tree and waited for the crowd of mourners to arrive. It was one o'clock and nobody was there yet.

Mr. Batman lay in state beside me. His open coffin was on a folding metal TV tray, with a pillowcase draped over the tray to make it look more like a dignified table.

I was wearing the cut-down black evening gown that I'd used for my bat costume the night I'd won Mr. Batman. It seemed only fitting. But since it was early April and kind of cold out, Mom made me wear my pink parka with the fur around the hood. On my feet were my orange rabbit slippers, because they looked like the deceased.

Finally the crowd started coming—Kimberley and Kirk, and Derek, who's younger than us and tags after us all the time. And somebody else. . . .

I squinted at the kid as he walked up the sidewalk toward us. It was the dirty little kid from the school bus. I didn't know how he'd heard about the funeral, but I didn't care. I was so glad to have anyone added to the crowd.

Mom couldn't come to the funeral because she was busy making the chocolate-cherry marble cake for afterwards. And Mrs. Birdsall waved at me from the window with her fingers pinching over her nose to show that her sinus was attacking her.

"You finally got here," I said to Kimberley and Kirk. "Here, Derek, you'll have to carry the shovel. Kimberley and I will be the pallbearers and carry the coffin. Kirk, you play some good funeral music. You—what's your name?"

The kid hung back and didn't answer.

"His name is Nick," Kirk said, "He just moved in over on Thirty-ninth Street someplace.

"Okay, Nick," I said. "You get to be the audience. You follow along after the coffin and mourn. Cry if you want to. Now, before we start for the cemetery, everybody has to pay their last respects to the deceased."

Derek went over and peered in at Mr. Batman. Kirk went over and took a quick look, like he wasn't much interested. Kimberley wouldn't go over till I gave her a crabby stare, then she glanced in.

"You're burying your Miss Piggy T-shirt? You're crazy, Zelda. That's your favorite shirt."

"If I gave him one I didn't want, that would be like Mom giving me a baking pan she didn't want anymore."

She didn't get it.

Nick, the dirty kid, took a good long look at Mr. Batman, and when his face came up it had tears on it. I was so glad he'd come!

"Okay now," I said, "time for the procession. First Kirk playing the music, then me and Kimberley with the coffin, then Nick, then Derek with the shovel. Got that? Ready? Okay, let's go."

We got lined up in the middle of the street and started marching. Kirk began to play.

"Whoa," I yelled, and stopped walking. "Kirk, that isn't a funeral song. That isn't any song at all. All it is is notes with holes in between."

"Shows how much you know. That is 'The Soldiers March.' "

"But it doesn't have any tune to it."

"It does too. Only the French horn doesn't carry the tune. It's just the counterpoint."

"Well, can't you play the tune part? We can't march to that."

He turned and explained, like he was talking to a little child, "The tune part has to be played by the cornets and the flutes. If we had any cornets and flutes, we could have the tune. The French horn plays the bottom line, and that's what I'm playing, and that's all you get."

I sighed.

We marched on. The French horn went *toot toot*, *toooooot*, and then a long space, and *toot toot, tooooot* again, only on two different notes. It was the most boring music I'd ever heard.

Down through the trailer park we went, past the community building and the picnic table and the three empty lots at the end. Then, across a little weedy ditch and into a field. It had bumpy ground and short shaggy grass that would turn into head-high weeds later in the summer. I was having some trouble keeping my slippers on, and my evening gown kept snagging on the weeds.

"Over there by that little tree," I said.

When we stopped, I took the shovel and started to dig the grave.

"No, no, Zelda," Kirk said, taking the shovel out of my hands. "You're doing it all wrong. You don't hit at the ground that way—you put your foot on the top of the shovel and push it in. And you can't do it with those stupid rabbit slippers on your feet."

He started digging, and in just a few digs he had a good grave.

"Not too deep," I told him. I didn't want Mr. Batman to have to work too hard when he rose.

We set the baking pan down in the hole, then stood around with our hands folded in front of us. Even Kimberley got into the spirit and did her part.

I stood at the head of the grave and said my speech. "Dearly beloved"—I didn't look at Nick—"we are gathered here to say good-bye to a fine guinea pig

by the name of Mr. Batman Hammersmith. He was loved by all who knew
him."

Kimberley coughed.

"He was loved by all who knew him,"
I yelled at her in a crabby voice.

"He was kind and generous and he
tried not to drop any guinea pig raisins
in my bed if he could possibly help it.
But sometimes he couldn't help it. But
he never bit anyone or did anything bad
in his whole life."

Kimberley snorted under her
breath.

"In his whole life since I had him,"
I snarled at her.

"So, good-bye, my dear darling Mr.
Batman, until we meet again."

He knew what I meant by that, even
if nobody else did.

I found some violets and sprinkled
them on top of the baking pan, then
Kirk started shoveling dirt in to fill the
grave. Derek and Kimberley were al-

ready halfway across the field toward the cake and pop.

Nick was still staring down at the grave, and he was crying again.

"Hey," I said to him. "That was really nice of you to come and cry for him. You didn't even know him."

He shook his head. "That's not why I'm crying," he said. It was the first time I'd heard his voice. It was a funny, low, croaky voice.

"Why are you?"

He kept looking down at the grave, where Kirk was finishing off with a few hard pats from the shovel.

" 'Cause you got to have a pet and I never did. You got to have him for a while, anyway."

He looked like he needed a hug pretty badly, so I gave him one.

◎

The next morning, I woke up early. It was as exciting as Christmas morning, almost. I got dressed without making any noise and went outside, zipping up my parka as I jumped down the steps.

I started toward the field, then went back and got the shovel out of the tool shed and took it along. Mr. Batman was going to have enough trouble rising from the baking pan without having to dig up through the dirt.

Unless he was out already!

I ran past the community building and the picnic table and the three empty lots at the end of the park. Over the ditch and into the field, turned left, to the grave over by the little tree.

Nope. He hadn't risen yet. The grave was still pounded smooth from Kirk hitting it with the back of the shovel. I sat down to wait.

I waited a very long time. The ground felt dry till I sat on it, but pretty soon my seat was damp and cold from the dirt.

"Here, Mr. Batman," I called softly.

The top of the grave didn't move.

Finally I decided I'd better help him. I dug the way Kirk showed me, but I couldn't get big bites of dirt to stay on the shovel the way he could. After about a hundred shovel shoves, there was the baking pan.

I got down on my knees and pulled off the lid.

He was still lying there, not looking anywhere near ready to get up and rise from the dead. If anything, he looked deader now than he had yesterday. I supposed being buried will do that to you.

For a very long, very long time I squatted there holding the baking pan lid and looking down at him. I knew he wasn't going to move and come back to life.

I was so mad.

I put the lid back on and pushed some dirt in the hole with my hands, and then I stood up and told Mr. Batman good-bye again. This time I really meant it.

I turned and walked home, dragging the shovel behind me.

◎

Mom gave me my usual basket of candy Easter eggs, then she made me get dressed up and go to church with her. I told her I was too mad about Mr. Batman to want to go sing songs to God.

"It won't do you any good to be mad at God," she said. "We have to have laws of nature, just like we have people laws. Otherwise the universe wouldn't work. It's the law of nature that everything has to die in order to make room for new everythings. You wouldn't want God to reach in and botch up the laws just because your pet's time came to die."

"Yes, I would," I growled as she herded me into the bathtub.

I sat all through church with my bottom lip stuck out. We didn't go to church very often, but every time we did, I had trouble with my feet. They would start swinging and kicking the seat in front of me, and I couldn't stop them. They'd wait till I was thinking about something else and then they'd start swinging. People in front were always turning around to frown at my legs.

Today I just sat like a rock. I didn't stand up to sing the hymns or anything. I didn't even look in the collection plate when it went by.

There were whole piles of flowers up in the front of the church, and most of the service was the choir singing songs like "There Was a New Jerusalem That Would Not Pass Away." Usually I loved that one, but today I was too mad and sad to let the music cheer me up.

Afer church we went home and had sloppy joes for lunch. Then Mom took the great big box of dyed Easter eggs that she'd been working on yesterday when she wasn't baking and serving cake. She met Mrs. Curtiss out in front, and a couple of the fathers, and they all headed toward the field to hide the eggs.

There was one golden egg on the top of the pile in the box. That was the important one. Find that and you'd win ten dollars. And be the biggest big shot at the hunt.

Thinking about it, I started getting happier and happier. All I had to do was win that ten dollars and I could buy a new guinea pig. Just like the laws of nature. The old had to make way for the new.

I still felt awful when I thought about the whisker-nose kisses, but it was exciting to think about picking out a new guinea pig and getting him trained to get under the covers.

While I waited for two o'clock, the time for the hunt, I went into my room and sat on the edge of my bed, looking down at the two cages. I'd have to clean the guinea pig cage really well for its new guinea pig.

I stuck my hand in with Bugs and rubbed him over his ears, but he didn't want to be rubbed. He kept standing up on his hind legs and biting at his stomach, as if he had a stomachache. He was even pulling mouthfuls of fur out of himself and making a mess in the cage.

Maybe he was missing Mr. Batman, too.

Finally it got to be time to go. I ran toward the field, getting more and more excited. This year I was really going to find the golden egg and win. And buy a new guinea pig.

At the edge of the field about twenty kids and their parents were standing around. Kimberley was still wearing her patent leather shoes and fancy dress, from church.

Ha, I thought. *You can't hunt eggs all dressed up.*

Kirk was pretty dressed up too. Ha at him.

"You don't have a chance, Zelda," he said to me.

"Ha."

I was glad to see Nick at the edge of the bunch. I thought he needed to have some fun.

One of the moms came along the line, giving each of us an empty Easter basket.

One of the dads yelled, "Okay now, all you kids get lined up here. Stay behind the ditch till I give the word. Then have at it. There are 101 Easter eggs in this field, 20 each of yellow, green, blue, pink, and purple, and 1 of gold. There will be a prize for whoever finds the most total eggs, for whoever finds the most of each of the five colors, and a grand prize for the finder of the golden egg."

Kirk looked at me. I gave him a silent *ha*.

The dad went on. "The boundaries are from the ditch to the fence over there, and from that row of bushes on the right to that big oak tree on the left. All right, everybody ready? On your mark . . ."

I got to the edge of the ditch.

"Get set . . ."

I got down in running position with my basket over my arm.

"Go!"

I leapt over the ditch and ran straight for the middle of the field. I figured most of the kids would start looking right there by the ditch, and I wanted to have the whole middle to myself.

A green egg!

A purple egg! And a yellow and a pink one right close together. They were all on the ground, tucked down into clumps of grass or bumpy places in the dirt.

I did a quick spin and almost fell over Nick. He'd tagged along right behind me. There were no eggs in his basket yet because my eagle eye kept seeing them before he did.

"Go over there by the fence," I told him. But he didn't go.

I snatched up two more green and a blue, but then I started thinking. The golden egg was the important one. The other prizes were just candy bars. And the golden egg was never just hidden in the grass like the others. It was always in a harder place.

I looked around. Fence posts, maybe. But Kirk was already over by the fence.

Then I thought of something. Still searching the grass as I went, I headed for Mr. Batman's grave, over at the edge of the boundaries.

I got to it and looked down. The hole was about half filled with the dirt I'd shoved in.

Way down in the dark part I saw a glint of gold.

Then I heard the weeds rustle, and turned around to look. Nick was standing beside me, looking up at me like he needed another hug.

I looked at him for the longest time.

I could still hear him saying he'd been crying because I'd had a pet for a little while and he never had.

I started to reach into the hole for the golden egg.

Nick was still looking up at me. I thought of something I did not want to think of. Ten dollars would buy a guinea pig for me. Or it would buy one for Nick.

Finally I took a deep breath and said, "Nick, why don't you check inside that hole? There might be an egg in there."

He shuffled over and started poking around in the pile of dirt that I hadn't put back into the grave.

I waited and waited while he poked around, but he wasn't getting the idea.

"Why don't you check down in the hole?" I said more firmly.

He closed his eyes and clutched his dirty hand down in the hole, but didn't touch anything.

"Oh, for Pete's sake, Nick," I yelled. "You have to open your eyes if you're going to find the golden egg."

Kirk was coming our way, with a hunter's gleam in his eye.

I grabbed Nick's wrist and jammed his hand down into the right end of the grave and held it there till the light came on in his face.

Nick was standing up, staring down at the golden egg in his hand, when Kirk came up.

"Ha," I said to him.

And Nick looked up with the biggest, dirtiest smile I'd ever seen. He didn't say anything, but there was a great big *ha* in his eyes.

◎

Mom and I walked into the trailer, tired but happy. I had my basketful of eggs and a giant 3 Musketeers bar for finding the most green eggs.

Mom put on her slippers and sat down at the card table in the living room, where she was halfway through a five-hundred-piece jigsaw puzzle that was driving her nuts because there were so many sky pieces.

I went into my room and stopped

dead in my tracks. There were little peeping noises coming from behind the bed.

I ran around and stared down into Bugs's cage. In one corner of the cage was a pile of pulled-out rabbit fur, and right in the middle of the fur were five little pink, naked, wiggling, squeaking THINGS.

I ran for Mom and dragged her away from her table, two sky pieces still in her hands.

"Bugs had babies," I breathed. "He had babies!"

"Well, Zelda, that's not entirely true." She looked at me and we both laughed.

"Okay, SHE had babies. THAT'S how Mr. Batman rose from the grave, Mom. I knew he'd figure out a way to do it. I knew he'd come back to me."

"Oh, whoa, dumpling." She sat down on the bed and wrapped her arm around me. "You think Mr. Batman has reincarnated himself as a rabbit?"

"I don't know what that means."

"Come back to life."

"Yes. One of those baby rabbits is him. Maybe all of them. I get to keep them, don't I, Mom? I do, don't I?"

She gave me a long, serious look. "Do you want a baby rabbit just because you think it's Mr. Batman come back to life?"

"I just want one. Or all."

"Honey, I don't think guinea pigs can come back to life as rabbits. I don't think it works that way."

"Do you know for sure?"

I had her there. She sidestepped the issue. "The rabbits belong to whoever Bugs belongs to . . . who obviously doesn't know a whole lot about rabbits if they couldn't tell a boy from a girl and didn't know she was going to have babies."

"She belongs to our room. To Mrs. Green, I guess. And Mrs. Green didn't even want one rabbit. She'll be glad to give me all the babies. She'll be thrilled to give me all the babies."

Mom sniffed and started to fight back a smile.

"You're probably right there, dumpling. Okay, let's put it this way. If Mrs. Green says it's okay, you may keep ONE of the babies. Only one, Zelda Marie. And no more of this nonsense about Mr. Batman coming back to life, okay?"

"Okay."

I sat watching the babies all the rest of the afternoon. It was very hard to tell from looking at them which one was a guinea pig on the inside. But I'd know it when the time came to choose.

Mr. Batman would find some way to let me know.

**F
HAL**

Hall, Lynn.

Here comes Zelda Claus, and other holiday disasters

$13.60

DATE DUE	BORROWER'S NAME	ROOM NO.
NOV 10 03	Jezaven	
DEC 16 03	Alayla	
JAN 05 04	Amiyah Funn	
	Dajanay Park er	2-201
	Sahanna Brown	2-201

**F
HAL**

Hall, Lynn.

Here comes Zelda Claus, and other holiday disasters

PS 309
SCHOOL LIBRARY